Emma's Vacation

Emma's Vacation

by David McPhail

Dutton Children's Books
New York

The author wishes to thank
John O'Connor for his help.

Copyright © 1987 by David McPhail

All rights reserved.

Unicorn is a registered trademark
of Dutton Children's Books.

Library of Congress number 86-24066
ISBN 0-525-44737-7

Published in the United States by
Dutton Children's Books,
a division of Penguin Books USA Inc.
375 Hudson Street
New York, New York 10014

Editor: Ann Durell

Printed in Hong Kong by South China Printing Co.
First Unicorn Edition 1991
10 9 8 7 6 5 4 3 2

Emma and her mother and father were
going on vacation.

It was a long ride.

Getting lost made the ride even longer.

When they finally got there, it was raining.

The roof of the cabin leaked in some places.

In the morning, the sun was shining.
Emma wanted to climb a mountain.

"We'll drive," said her father.

They went out to lunch.

They rode on a boat and a bus…

and a train

and a rocket ship.

The next day, Emma wouldn't budge.
"I want to stay here," she said.

"Here?" said her mother and father. "What can we do here?"

"We can wade in the brook," said Emma,

"and try to catch a fish."

"We can pick some berries

and climb a tree."

"We can pack a picnic and go for a hike.

When we get back, we can lie in the
hammock and sing songs and tell stories."

Emma was having a wonderful vacation.